2 bunny rabbits

3 chirping birds

  Tweet. Tweet.

4 wild mushrooms

5 colorful trees

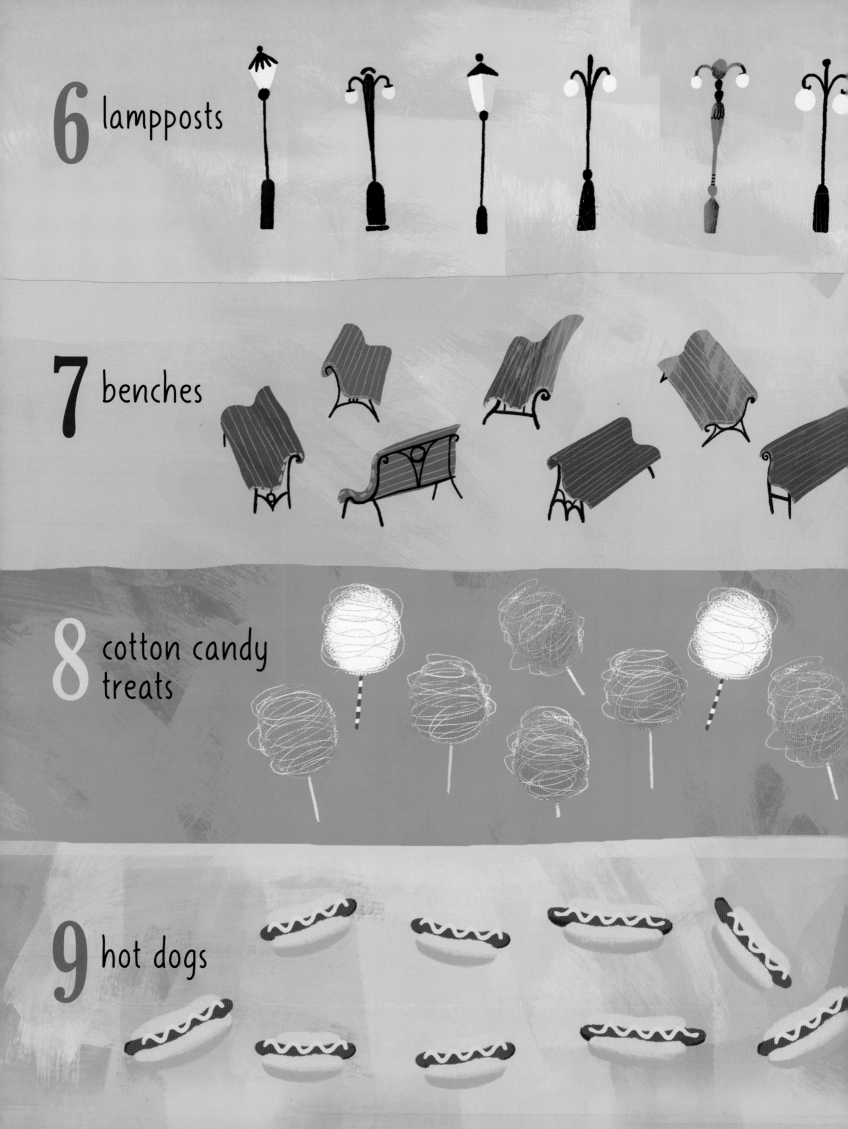

6 lampposts

7 benches

8 cotton candy treats

9 hot dogs

10 people in the park

You did it!
Turn the page
and count to **20**.

20 boats

There are so many kinds of seaworthy vessels. Count them from **1** to **20**.

Find the hidden octopus.

Follow the anchor lines to their ships.

Find the two striped rowboats.

40 animals

It's snack time for these animals.
Count them from **1** to **40**.

50 vegetables

Welcome to the vegetable garden!
Count them from 1 to 50.

Point to all
the rabbits.

Follow the maze
to help the dog
find his bone.

START

Find the hidden bird.
FINISH
squeak!
Count all the cabbages. Then, count all the pumpkins.

70 snowflakes

Snowflakes are falling in this winter wonderland! Count them from 1 to 70.

How many holly berries are there?

Hello!

Which animal made these tracks?

Find the pink snowflake.

Find **6** differences between the snowmen.

90 buttons

Buttons come in all shapes, sizes, and colors!
Count them from 1 to 90.

How many buttons have **4** holes?

Find the button with a heart on it.

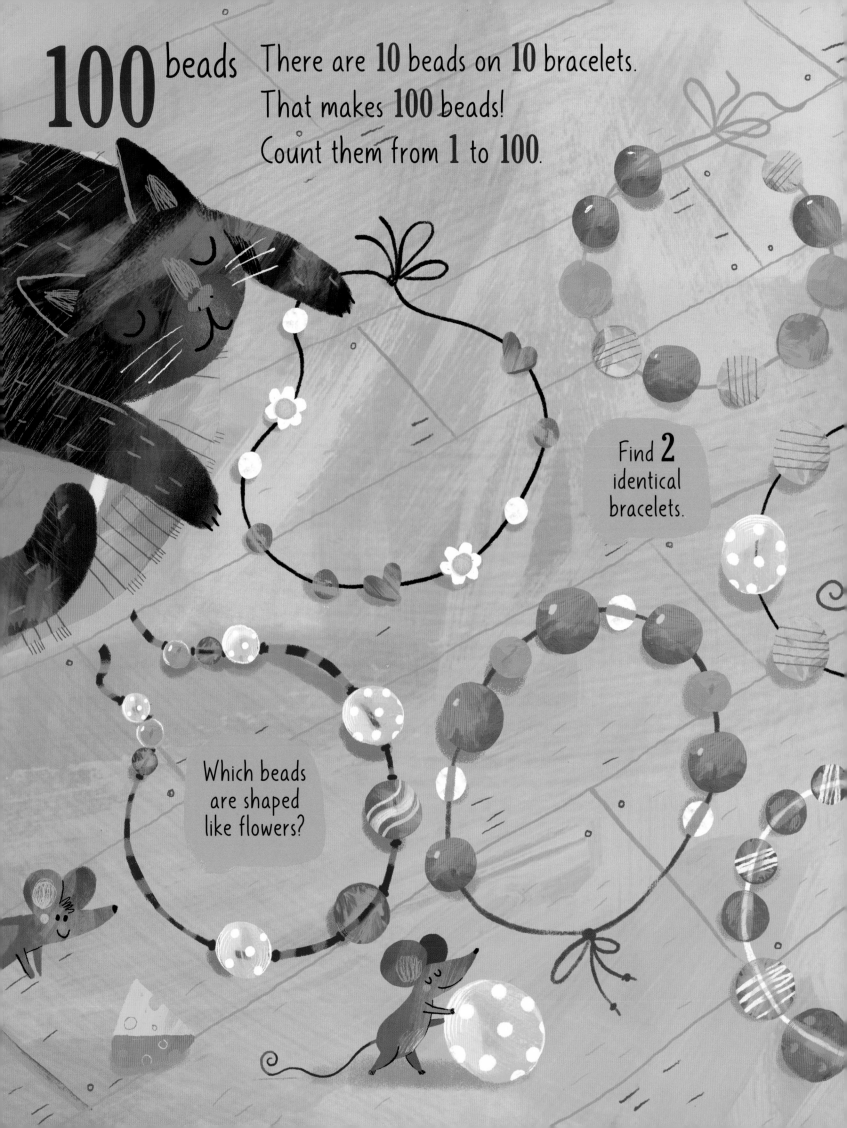

100 beads

There are **10** beads on **10** bracelets.
That makes **100** beads!
Count them from **1** to **100**.

Find **2** identical bracelets.

Which beads are shaped like flowers?